Trees

Trees

By Lucy Hemphill
Illustrations by Michael Joyal

Winnipeg

Trees

Copyright © 2022 Lucy Hemphill
Illustrations copyright © 2022 Michael Joyal

Design and layout by Matthew Stevens and M. C. Joudrey.

Published by At Bay Press September 2022.

All rights reserved. The use of any part of this publication, reproduced, transmitted in any form or by any means electronic, mechanical, photocopying, recording or otherwise, or stored in a retrieval system without prior written consent of the publisher or in the case of photocopying or other reprographic copying, license from the Canadian Copyright Licensing Agency-is an infringement of the copyright law.

No portion of this work may be reproduced without express written permission from At Bay Press.

Library and Archives Canada cataloguing in publication is available upon request.

ISBN 978-1-988168-28-9

Printed and bound in Canada.

This book is printed on acid free paper that is 100% recycled ancient forest friendly (100% post-consumer recycled).

This book was made with the generous support of the Manitoba Arts Council and the Canada Council for the Arts.

MANITOBA ARTS COUNCIL   CONSEIL DES ARTS DU MANITOBA

Canada Council for the Arts   Conseil des arts du Canada

First Edition

10 9 8 7 6 5 4 3 2 1

atbaypress.com

For the Gwa'sala-'Nakwaxda'xw, my community and family, who despite everything maintain deep roots and stay strong together in all we do.

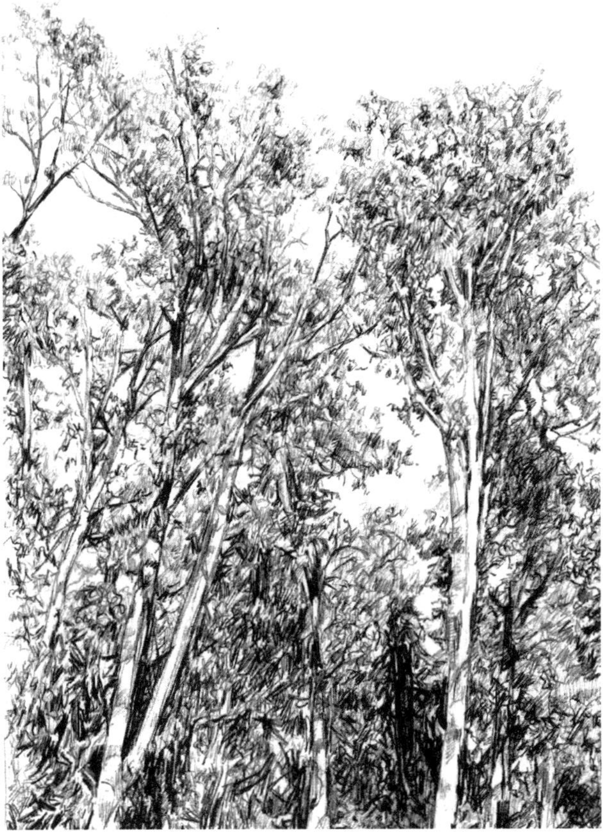

The steady drumbeat of my pulse punctuates the whirr of the engine, the crackle of the radio and the pilot's jarring voice barely audible as we fly over the Charlotte Straight. The pilot looks at me nervously as I gasp for air. The flight over is only a thirty-minute trip, but time has slowed down for me. I unconsciously hold my breath in anticipation of what I will find. It's been too long since I was last home, and I'm returning to gather plant medicines for my community.

Beneath the wisps of early morning fog, the silver sea glitters where the sun caresses its surface. The territories of the Gwa'sala-'Nakwaxda'xw span Smith Inlet, Seymore Inlet, Blunden Harbour, and some of the islands between the mainland of what are now called British Columbia and Vancouver Island. These vast territories were never signed over to Canada in treaties, nor were they lost in war.

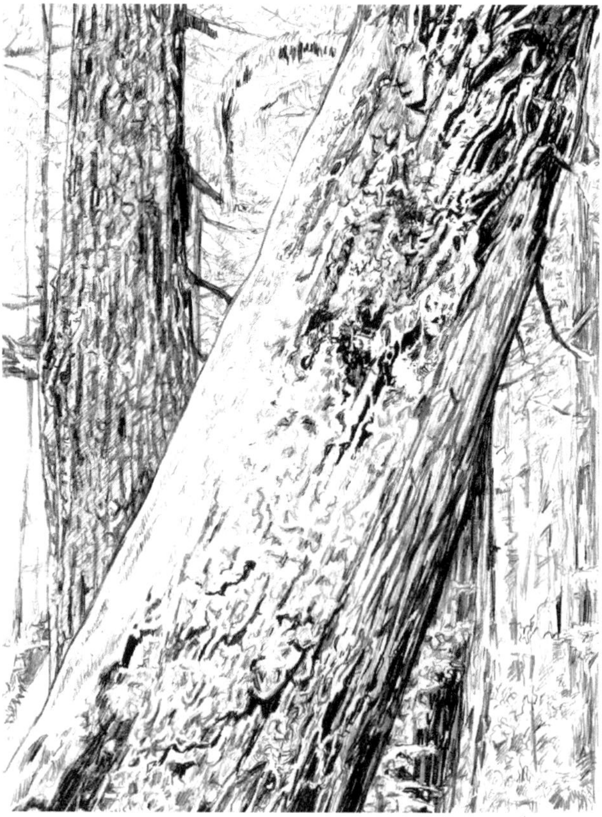

At first glance it seems as if there is nothing in our territories but forest and sea. But as the plane crosses the straight, and begins to pass over the inlets, I can see that much has changed since I was last here. Where once there were vast green swaths of trees covering every piece of land, now there are great brown patches where the old growth has been completely cut down. Mountains are marked with the scars of landslides where tree roots no longer hold the land to the rock face. Rivers and inlets are dammed with the wreckage of entire forests.

As we fly over clear-cut, after clear-cut, after clear-cut, I double over as if being punched in the stomach. When the plane lands on calm, dark water, I gather the scattered pieces of my mind and breathe in the air of my territories. The salt of tears stings my cheeks, but I walk straight into the forest before anyone can see my swollen and sad eyes. I have come home to find medicine and there is no time to waste.

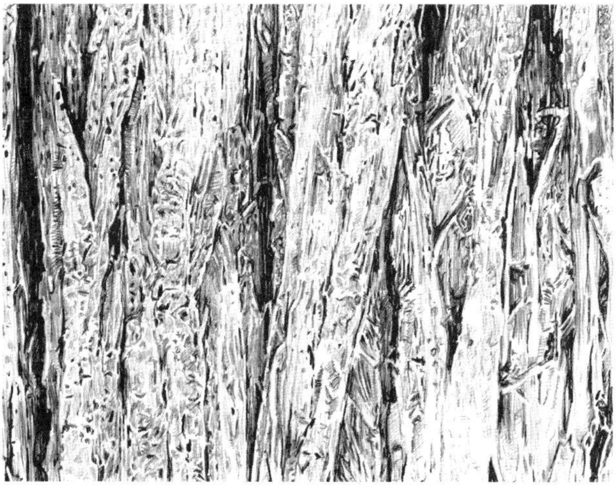

As I slip through a veil of tangled waxy nak̓waḻ'mas leaves and into the canopy of the a'tłi, I pause so that my eyes can adjust to the darkness. I breathe in the rich earthiness of lichen, soil, fungi and trees. In the shelter of the a'tłi, I feel comforted, and my strength returns as I begin to walk.

The large, grey-scaled trunks of a̱li'was trees are all around me. I can smell the sharp resinous pitch oozing from places the trees have been wounded by dładłana̱'eł and winter storms. I've been told that a̱li'was pitch is one of the first medicines of the Kwakwaka'wakw. Long ago, we were taught to use it on our wounds by our relative, the ga̱la. I have even seen giga̱la, at Na̱ḵił- the head of Smith Inlet, rubbing their wounds on the sticky sap dripping from wounded trees.

The fragrance of the sap recalls a memory: I was eight years old and I was at a kwak'wala language camp with my family. My sister fell out of a bunk bed and split her top lip with her braces. After being rushed to the hospital for stiches, she was told that she would have a large and unsightly scar. Wa'ta, a Kwakwaka'wakw Elder and medicine woman at the camp gave her a spruce-pitch ointment. After applying the medicine twice each day, my sister's wound healed well, and didn't scar. That was when I started to understand the magic contained within the trees. It was the beginning of my relationship-building journey which, in many ways, has brought me to this a'tłi now.

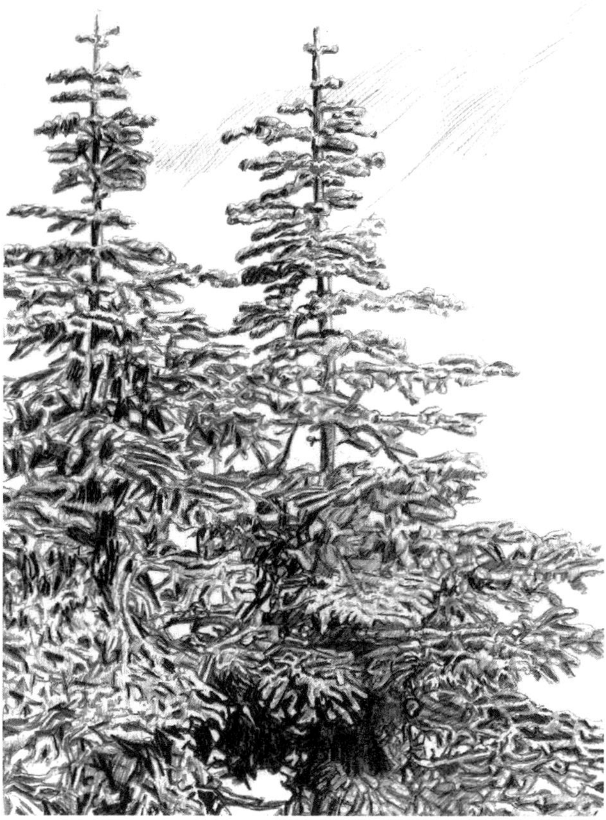

I look down at the moss carpeting of the forest floor that gently cradles my boot, springing back with each step. When I look back in the direction from which I came, the faint outline of my steps remains on the forest floor. I wonder if this moss holds the memories of my ancestors who walked this same forest, perhaps in search of the same medicines I am looking for now.

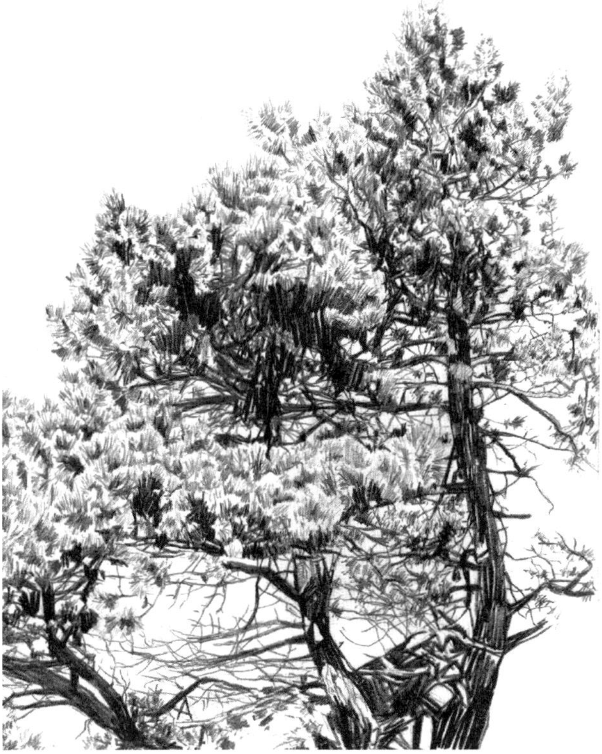

In 1964 the Canadian government forcefully relocated my people – The Gwa'sala and 'Nakwaxda'xw'– from these territories to a small village called Tsulquate, in the territories of the Kwagu'ł on Vancouver Island. Both tribes arrived to only three houses built on the Tsulquate reserve, and nowhere to moor their boats. Many tried to return to our villages, but when they went back, they found that government workers had burnt their homes to the ground. As a child, I remember visiting the old village sites with my family and seeing the charred and decomposing cedar pillars of gukwdzi being reclaimed by the land that held them; symbols of life before the relocation.

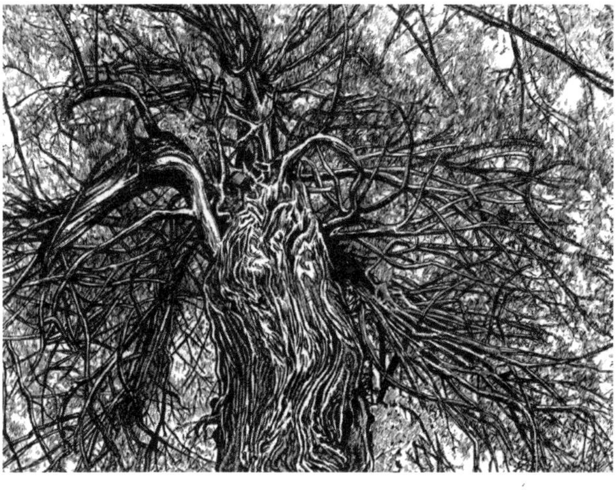

Our way of life required us to have an intimate relationship with the land and the sea. But few returned after the relocation. Gwa'sala and 'Nakwaxda'xw' children were forced to attend residential schools. The natural transmission of sacred and ancestral knowledge was disrupted. As a child I remember feeling the heavy cloak of shame carried by every Gwa'sala-'Nakwaxda'xw person I knew. Only the old ones, the ones who lived in our territories before the relocation, could speak our language. As our language was formed in relationship to the same land and waterways we were torn from, it's no wonder we've forgotten how to speak it.

The story of the Gwa'sala-'Nakwaxda'xw relocation is not unique. I have heard stories of many other Indigenous people being forced from their territories with every attempt made to assimilate them into a culture that had no value for rooted people. Being rooted means it is harder to take the land from beneath you.

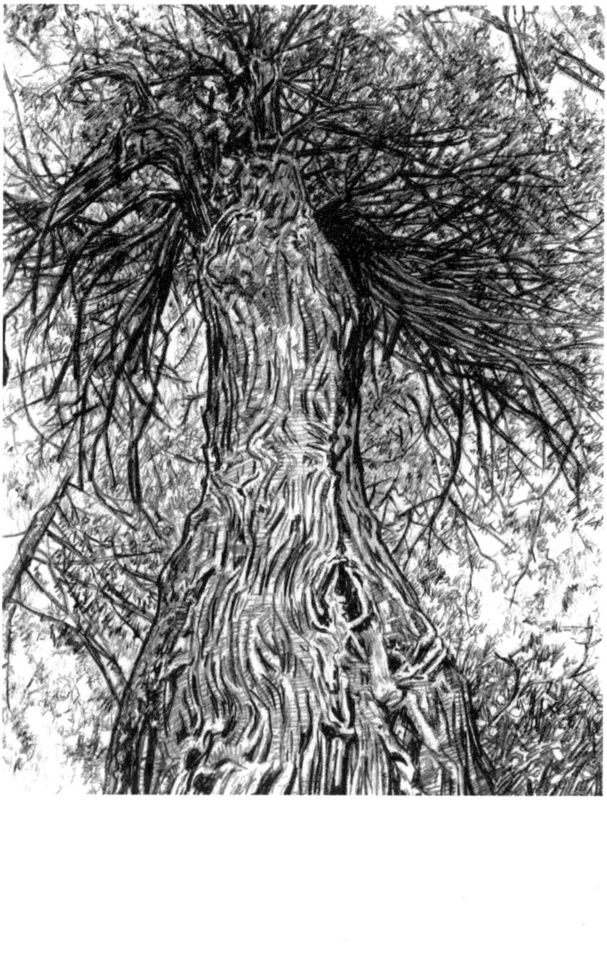

A beam of golden sunlight pulls me from my thoughts and I notice a hole in the a'tɬi canopy. A great ancient ali'was has fallen. Many plants are thriving here that would otherwise struggle to grow in the dark undergrowth. *"hamxitlan tlaxa gwadam,"* I whisper, before I stop to eat some juicy gwadam. The words of my ancestors form clumsily in my lazy mouth, and yet, speaking them feels truer than English ever has.

As the tart berries further restore my body and spirit, I regard the ancient one before me. This ali'was must have fallen some time ago, because it has become a nursery log, with three young loxw'mas trees growing up from its fallen body. I am moved by the way this old one, even in death, continues to provide for the young trees and plants around it.

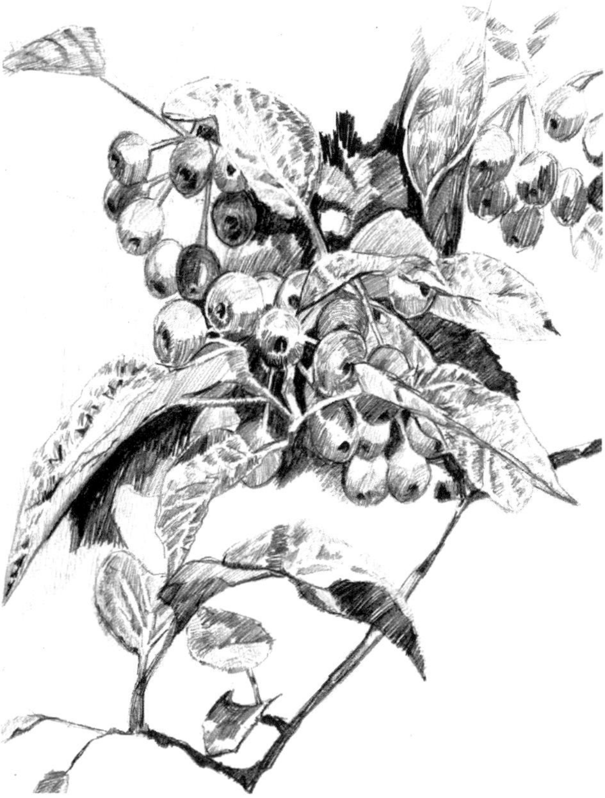

The Canadian government sought to fracture family structures so that many forgot how to maintain the reciprocal relationships so important to us. Families were forced to move from cedar gukwdzi to lino single-family homes that were not built to last, and quickly filled with mold, poisoning lungs just as minds were poisoned with despair, resentment and shame. Few returned to our homelands, and those who did, took what they could – trees, salmon, minerals – to be sold off for a price in a capitalist, colonial society. Residential schools made every attempt to teach our grandparents, aunts, uncles and parents to forget the meaning of love and connection. And every aspect of the society we were meant to now participate in went against our teachings of reciprocity and care.

I can hear my heartbeat drumming in my ears again, as I reach down and pick up a fallen ali'was branch.

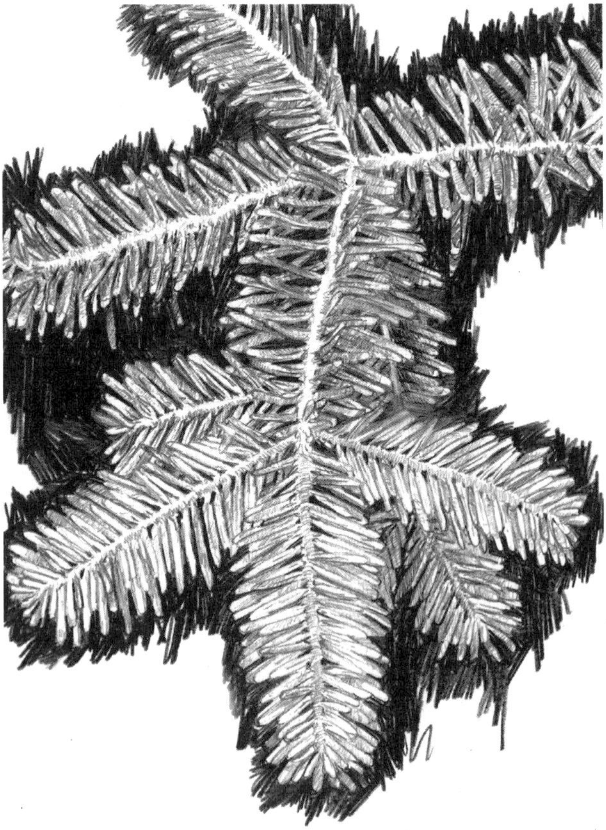

My hands gently cradle the sharp bristles. For so long we have carried the heavy burden of living in a world built on the destruction of our own. A heaviness like this seems insurmountable.

For the Kwakwaka'wakw, ali'was is a strong cleansing medicine. It can be used in ceremonial cleansing to scrub away the heaviest, darkest and most painful burdens. It's also believed to cleanse away black magic. When I was pregnant with my son, I was a student in an academic institution that had no use for a Kwakwaka'wakw single mother. I returned to Tsulquate because I needed my family and my community. I needed to be near my territories so that I could strengthen my roots before my son arrived. I knew I needed to be strong for him. I was alone and afraid, and I turned to ali'was to take away the heaviness I carried. I cleansed with the spiky boughs weekly, and slowly the heaviness left me until I was ready to prepare myself for my son's birth, and for my role as his mother.

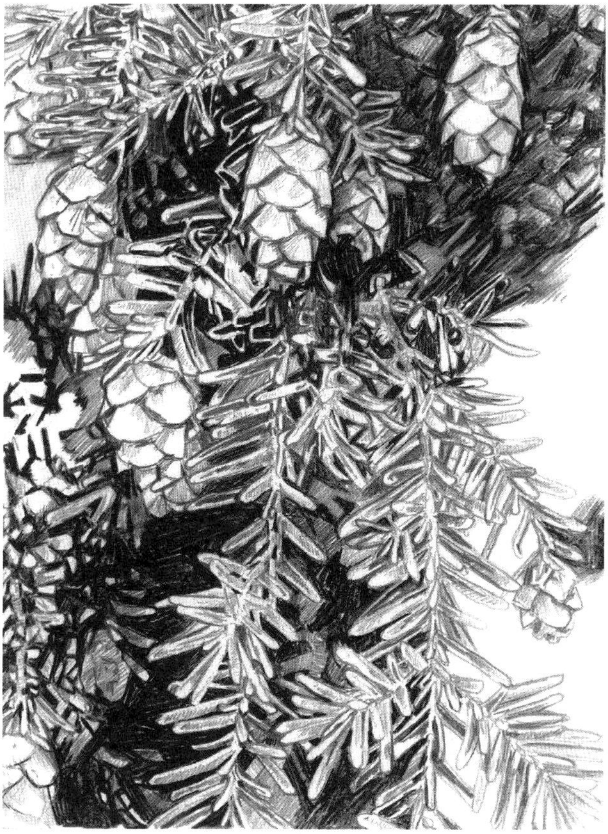

In the distance I can hear what sounds like the echo of water droplets. I smile, recognizing the call of gwa'wina. I look up, and I am startled to see a great wilkw with a long, white strip of bare flesh where the bark has been removed. The bark is rounded and bulging inwards over the strip where the tree has been healing itself for at least a hundred years. It was likely removed by my ancestors, possibly to be used in the tseka. The Kwakwaka'wakw sustainably harvested what they needed from trees without killing them. They even removed slabs of wood to build their homes from living trees. They knew how much could be taken while allowing the tree to continue to live.

Not long ago, researchers studied culturally modified trees such as this one. They learned that the trees went through a period of enhanced growth after being harvested, which confirms what my ancestors already knew: harvesting in a respectful way that maintained a reciprocal relationship ensured that there would be more for future generations, not less. Wilkw is vital to the building and thriving of our communities, culture and ceremonies. The tree of life gave us everything that was needed, and my ancestors never took the wilkw for granted.

I reach out and caress the bare flesh of the wilkw, then rest my hand against the soft and fibrous bark. "G̱ilakas'la," I whisper, as I am overcome with gratitude for the gift this tree gave to my people.

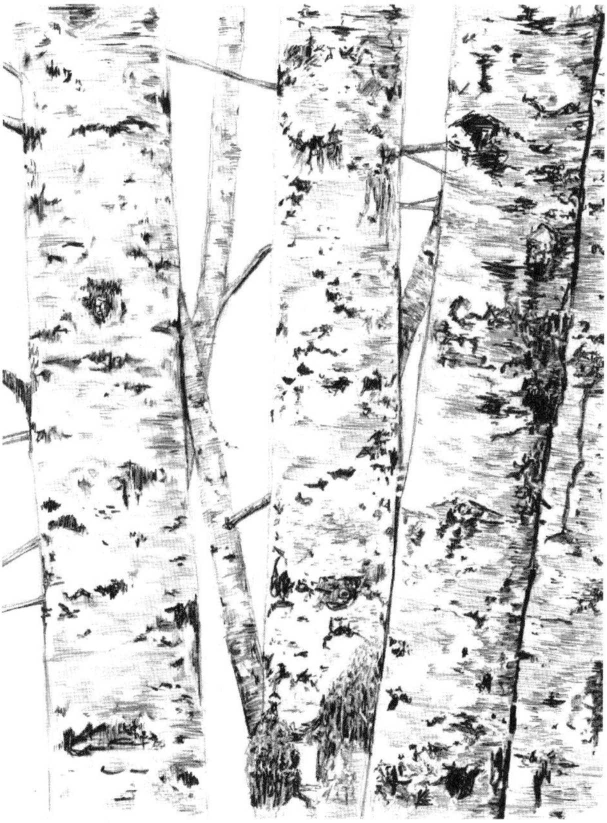

The t̓sek̲a is a sacred ceremony carried out in the potlatch. It begins with four chiefs holding a circle of red cedar bark around a matriarch from the potlatching family. After the chiefs and matriarch circle the floor four times, one of the chiefs tries to sever the cedar bark ring. He strikes three times but does not sever the ring until the fourth strike. At that time, the young women of the family distribute red cedar bark strips for all to wear for the duration of the t̓sek̲a. The cedar bark keeps guests safe from the spirit realm while they witness the ceremony.

In my family, as with many among the Kwakwaka'wakw, our matriarchs kept our ceremonies and stories alive. They nurtured the reciprocal relationships that were integral to who we are. Like the tree of life, the matriarchs were, and still are, the pillars of our families and society. Like the cedar tree, they have given and continue to give generously. My drive to be in our homelands to do this work of medicine gathering is a direct result of the efforts of my mother, aunts, grandmother and great grandmothers. I am here because of them.

I breathe deeply, and the invigorating smell of fresh green tsapax̱ causes everything to feel sharper and more alive as I look around at the trees surrounding me. There are many great wilkw; some so big that if I was to lay at their base, curled around the trunk, I would not reach one quarter of their circumference. Yet there are danas'mas too, along with ali'was, and much smaller loxw'mas. These trees thrive in community, together with many other plants and fungi.

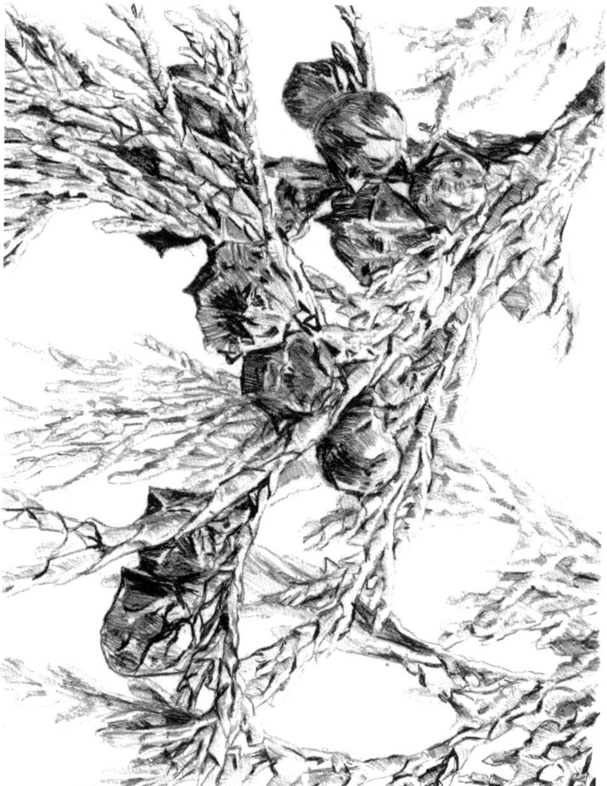

When a forest is clear-cut, the forestry company replaces the trees they cut down with whichever species of tree is the most profitable at the time. Often, these are wilkw trees. The baby wilkw are given everything that the forestry companies believe they need: fertilizer, sunshine, rain and space to grow. And they do grow.

In fact, they grow very fast. Each tree looks almost exactly like the next. Yet, when the trees are cut down, the loggers find that many are hollow inside. They grow too fast, and too efficiently without the shelter from their parent and grandparent trees. The trees look perfectly healthy from the outside, but without the nurture and protection of their family and community, they are hollow inside.

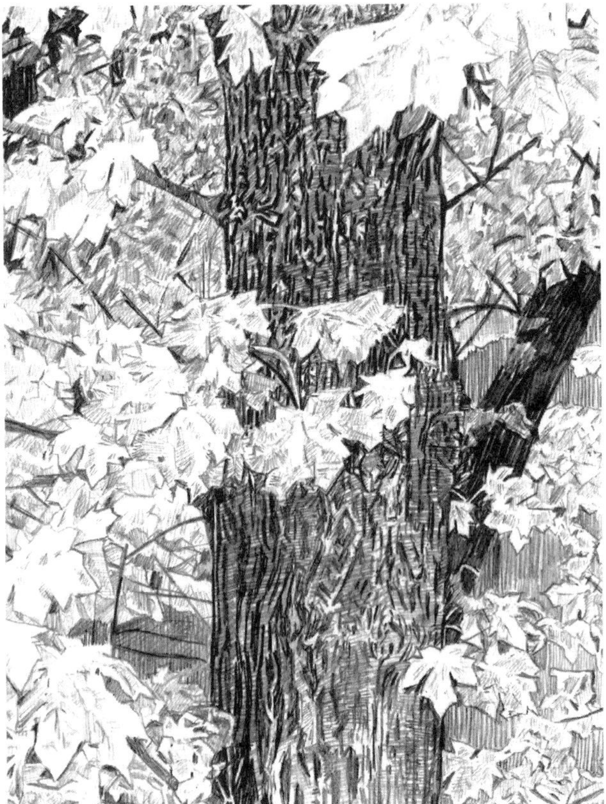

As I recall the clear-cuts, anger begins to thrash around in my belly, making me feel seasick. Feathery loxw'mas boughs brush my face, bringing me back to the forest. I reach my arms out and grasp the loxw'mas tree to stabilize myself. I thank the tree for her gentle gift.

Anger may help dismantle the destructive systems that make every attempt to destroy us, and heaviness may help us learn how to grow roots. But loxw'm a̱s reminds us that we can't accomplish either without the presence of gentleness. Gentleness for ourselves, and for our communities as we collectively heal and dream our way back to a world more aligned with who we are.

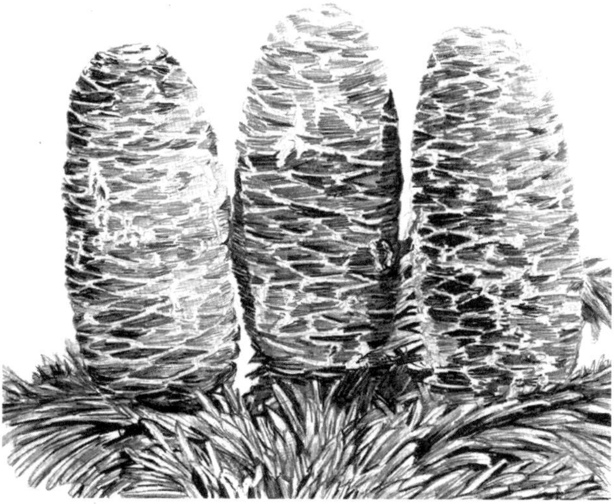

As a child I would make beds from loxw'mas branches and lay in the soft feathery boughs of what I later learned was another powerful medicine for my people. She is gentle, but her gentleness is her strength. She guards our doorways to the spirit realm. The boughs of fresh, fragrant loxw'mas are placed around the doors of our gukwdzi and around the entrance to the dance floor in our potlach ceremonies. Loxw'mas is a powerful cleansing medicine and is used in initiation ceremonies for our dancers. Not only does it cleanse, but it also enables only that which we choose to come in from the spirit realm, and nothing else. In this way, we stay connected to the stories and the gifts of our ancestors, without allowing the heaviness of hundreds of years of colonization and trauma to also come through.

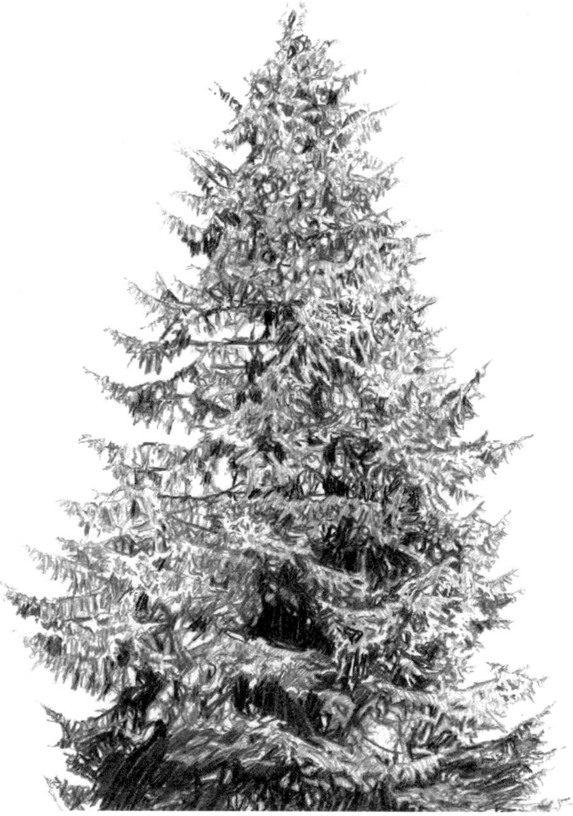

Before my son was born, I wanted to connect to the birthing practices of my ancestors, but it was difficult to find information. My grandmother and aunts had not felt safe enough to turn to our traditional birthing practices. Many others had also turned away from our birthing practices, afraid that their babies would be taken away if they did. So, sadly, that sacred knowledge was not passed on. While I was pregnant with my son, I prayed for the knowledge and strength to carry him into this world in a good way.

A month before he was born, I dreamt that my family prepared for his arrival by ceremonially sweeping our homes and the delivery room with loxw'm̲as boughs. Later, my mother and sister carried this out for me, before I gave birth. They even placed the loxw'm̲as bows at the doorway to the delivery room, in the same way we do when we conduct our ceremonies in the gukwdzi. And so, my son entered our world in a good way.

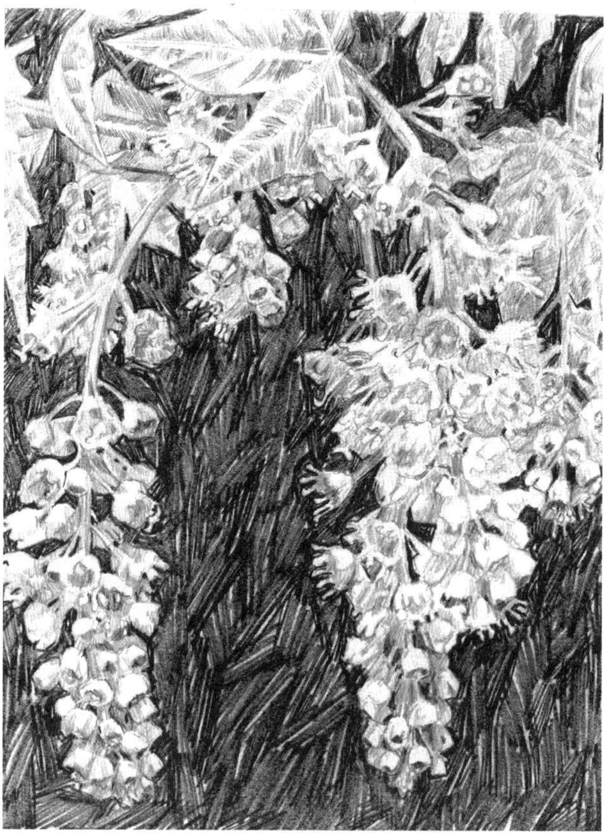

As I gaze around the a'tłi, I notice that most of the young trees are loxw'mas. Here, in the dark undergrowth, these soft and fragrant trees are thriving. Ahead of me, I see the golden light of the sun again. As I step out of the lush green a'tłi, my foot leaves the gentle moss and lands on scorched ground. But my step does not falter. As I look out over the expansive clear-cut, I see the stumps of the trees that once dwelled here. But I also see the pink cotton-candy blooms covering the blackened earth.

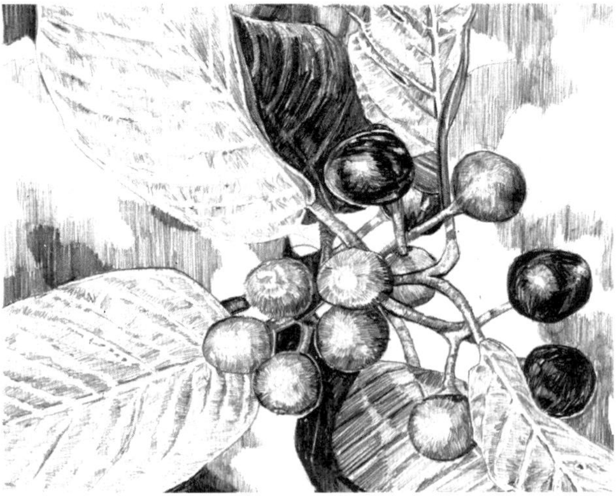

Gwagwaltama seeds travel on the wind, and settle into the ground, preparing the earth so that other plant life can thrive here. They bloom, provide food for bees and birds, and then put nutrients into the ground. Soon, trees spring up where their seeds had been hidden in the earth. In this way, gwagwaltama begin the process of forest regeneration.

Our Indigenous languages, identity and cultures, were formed in relationship to the land and waterways which we come from. We were never meant to exist separately from them. I once asked my dear friend, Pepakiye, why we find such vibrant and powerful medicines in clear-cuts, places seemingly left barren by the destruction of capitalistic greed. She replied, "Medicines and prayers from our ancestors are stored in the land, even after it has been destroyed."

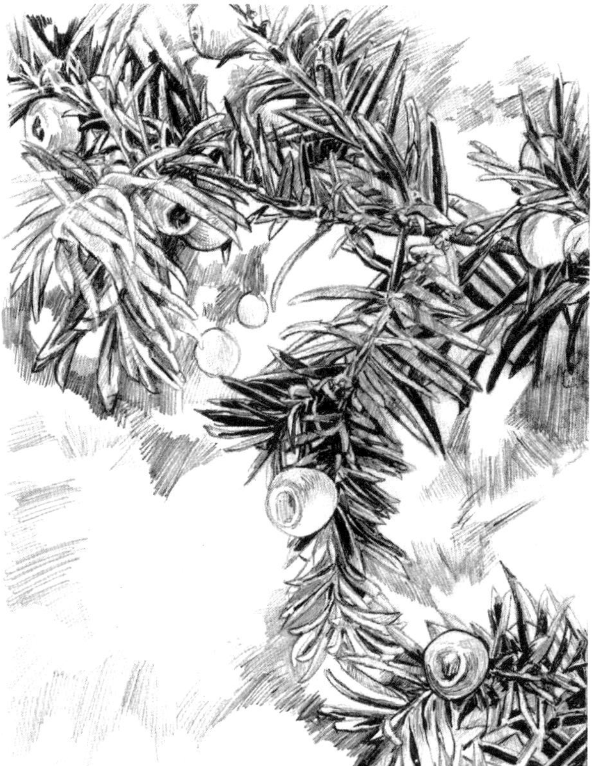

From the outside looking in, maybe it looks like we have been assimilated into Canadian society. Maybe it looks like we've lost everything.

But the truth is, our ancestors' prayers are held within us, the same way they are held in the land and waterways we come from. These prayers awaken, the more we heal, the more we support each other and the more we build relationships to the places we come from.

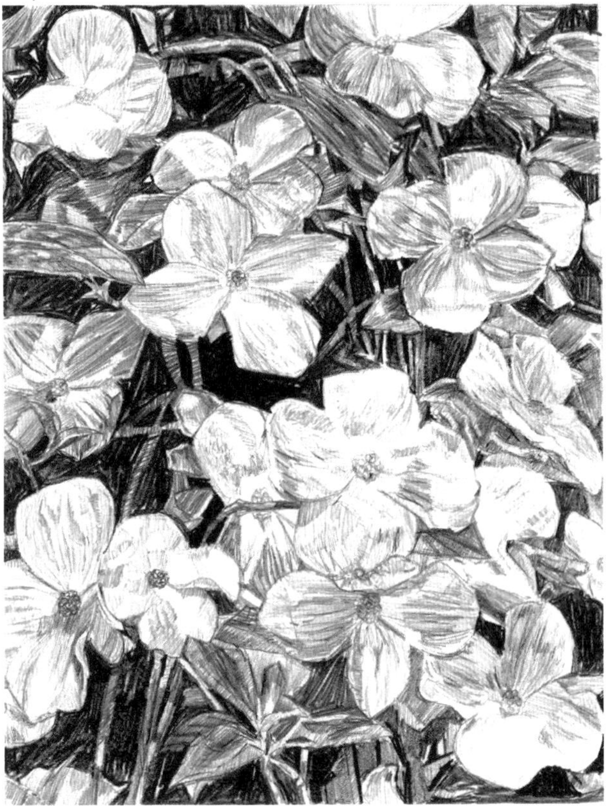

When we blossom together, caring for one another and holding each other up, we are healing ourselves, and we are healing the land. We go within to heal, and we emerge ready to grow our worlds once again. We are preparing for the regeneration of our a'tłi.

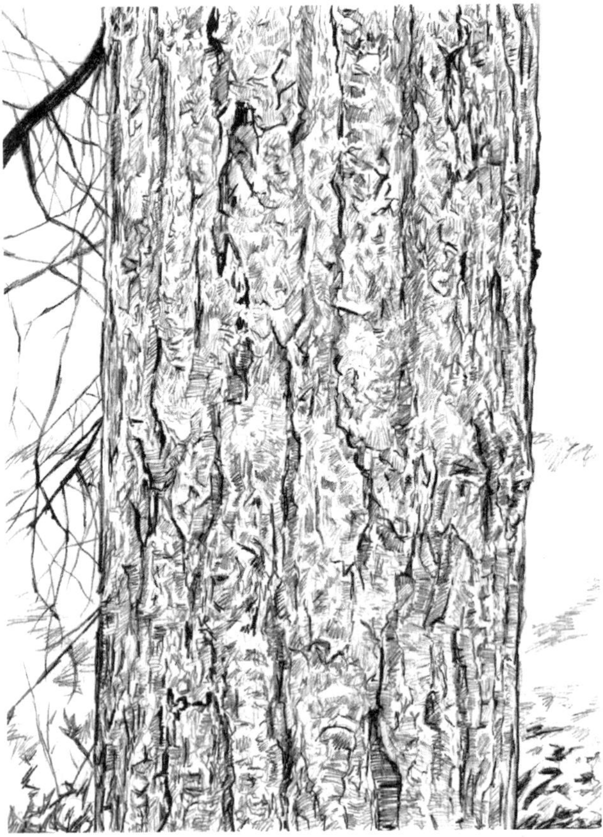

I travelled to my homelands to find medicine to bring back to my people, but we have been carrying the medicine within us all along. I kneel down and look closely at the blackened earth between the aromatic stalks of gwagwaltama. I can see fresh green seedlings, tiny windmills emerging through the soil.

I remember the time before I gave birth to my son, when I did not have a name for him. But the moment he entered our world, I knew his name could only be
        A̱li'was.

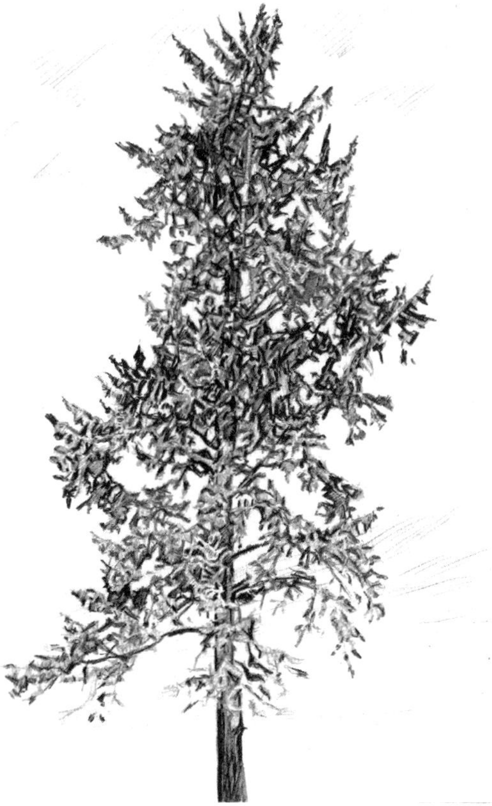

Glossary: Dendrological Illustrations

Page 1   - Red Adler - Alnus rubra

Page 4   - Pacific Yew - Taxus brevifolia

Page 7   - Western Red Cedar - Thuja plicata

Page 11 - Amabalis Fir - Abies amabilis

Page 13 - Shore Pine - Pinus contorta

Page 15 - Western Red Cedar - Thuja plicata

Page 18 - Western Red Cedar - Thuja plicata

Page 21 - Pacific Crab Apple - Malus fusca

Page 24 - Grand Fir - Abies grandis

Page 27 - Western Hemlock - Tsuga heterophylla

Page 31 - Red Alder - Alnus rubra

Page 35 - Western Red Cedar - Thuja plicata

Page 38 - Big Leaf Maple - Acer macrophyllum

Page 41 - Amabalis Fir - Abies amabilis

Page 43 - Western Hemlock - Tsuga heterophylla

Page 46 - Big Leaf Maple - Acer macrophyllum

Page 48 - Cascara - Rhamnus purshiana

Page 51 - Pacific Yew - Taxus breviofolia

Page 54 - Pacific Dogwood - Cornus nuttallii

Page 56 - Western Hemlock - Tsuga heterophylla

Page 59 - Sitka Spruce - Picea sitchensis

Kwak̓wala Words

Gwa'sala-'Nakwaxda'xw [gwah-sah-lah-nak-wak-tow]
Two Kwakwaka'wakw tribes who were forcefully relocated from their traditional territories by the Canadian government in 1964. They were amalgamated and are now considered one Tribe.

nak̓wal'mas [Nah-kwulth-mas]
Salal plant

a'tłi [ah-tlee]
Forest

ali'was [Uh-lee-wass]
Sitka spruce tree

dładłana'eł [Dlah-dlah-nah-elth]
Woodpecker

Kwakwaka'wakw [kwah-kwuh-kyuh-wakw]
Meaning: "kwak̓wala speaking people." A group of distinct First Nations tribes who live on the central coast of British Columbia, including north Vancouver Island and mainland BC and speak different dialects of the kwak̓wala language.

gala [Gyuh-lah]
Grizzly bear

Nakił [Nuh-keelth]
Gwa'sala village, located along the Nekite River at the head of Smith Inlet, British Columbia.

kwak̕wala [kwah-kwal-ah], with an explosive second 'k'
The language spoken by the Kwakwaka'wakw
people. Due to colonization, forced relocation from land, and residential school, it is now considered an endangered language.

Wa'ta [Wah-tah]
Kwagu'ł Elder and medicine woman

Tsulquate [Tsul-qwa-tee]
Reserve near Port Hardy BC, in Kwagu'ł Territories, to which the Gwa'sala and 'Nakwaxda'xw were forcefully relocated by the Canadian Government in 1964.

Kwagu'ł [Kwa-gewlth]
One of the Kwakwaka'wakw tribes, whose traditional territories are located on the east coast of North Vancouver Island, near Port Hardy, British Columbia, and near Queen Charlotte Straight.

gukwdzi [gewk-dzee]
Traditional Kwakwaka'wakw cedar bighouse

gwadam [gwah-duhm]
Huckleberries

loxw'mas [loxw-muhs]
Hemlock tree

g̱wa'wina [gwah-ween-ah], with the first 'g' sounded at the back of the throat
raven

wilkw [wilkw]
Red cedar tree

t'sek̲a [tsay-kah], with an explosive 'ts'
Red cedar bark ceremony, held during a potlatch.

g̲ilakas'la [Gee-lah-kas-lah], with the first 'g' sounded at the back of the throat
a greeting and also means thank you.

t'sap'ax̲ [tsa-pax], with an explosive 'ts' and 'p' and a guttural 'x'
cedar leaves

da̲nas'ma̲s [Duh-nas-muhs]
small cedar tree

gwagwa̲ltama [Gwa-gwuhl-tama]
Fireweed

About the Author

Lucy Hemphill, writer and adventurer of Kwakwaka'wakw/Métis and Scottish/Irish descent. She is a member of the Gwa'sala-'Nakwaxda'xw Nations, a Kwakwaka'wakw Community on the northern tip of Vancouver Island, British Columbia. Much of her life has been spent in the forest or on the sea. When she's not surrounded by nature she writes about it. She also writes about contemporary and historical Indigenous issues.

About the Artist

Michael Joyal, Canadian watercolour artist whose work focuses on reinterpreting characters from mythology and fairy tales through a modern lens. His paintings explore roles of feminine power through feelings of strength, anger, melancholy and joy. He has exhibited in Canada and the United States. His work is held in permanent collection at the International Cryptozoology Museum and the Legislative Library of Manitoba. To view more of his art, visit leadvitamins.com

Thanks for purchasing this book and for supporting authors and artists. As a token of gratitude, please scan the QR code for exclusive content from this title.